FOR JASIEK AND MARIANKA

DESIGN

※ DOMESTIC EQUIPMENT: SLEEK, INGENIOUS,
GROUNDBREAKING, NOTEWORTHY

TEXT:
EWA SOLARZ

ILLUSTRATIONS:
ALEKSANDRA AND DANIEL MIZIELIŃSKI

TRANSLATION:
ELŻBIETA WÓJCIK-LEESE

GECKO PRESS

Design* is the art of **inventing and creating objects**. It is coming up with ideas about what an object might be and how to produce it.

Take a look round your bedroom. Everything there has been designed: your bed, mattress, curtains, carpet, desk, chair, lamp, bookshelves, books, school bag, computer, crayons, pencil case ... Even that sweet wrapper on the floor, and the sweet itself.

Without design we would have hardly any manufactured objects. In order to produce something, we need to design that thing first. Good design happens when designers invent objects that are **practical, comfortable, easy to use, and attractive**. As you can see, the term 'design' means both the whole process and its outcome – a designed object.

* OTHERWISE KNOWN AS
'INDUSTRIAL DESIGN'

what is *D.E.S.I.G.N.?*

D.E.S.I.G.N. is a selection of **sixty-nine objects** created by the most influential and **famous designers** from around the world. Choosing these particular objects – and not others – was extremely difficult, because the history of design abounds in fascinating designs and excellent designers.

Designers can design almost anything. But not everything can be shown in one book. Here you will see only **things that can be found at home**: pieces of furniture, lamps and domestic gadgets. These objects are **presented chronologically** – from the oldest to the most recent.

SELECTED WORLD-FAMOUS
DESIGNERS
↓

can I buy these things?

Almost all the objects described in this book are still being produced, so you can definitely buy them. Be careful though – they may **cost you a fortune**! Because these things have been designed by some of the **best designers in the whole world**, they cost much more than objects created by lesser-known designers. The best designers are paid a lot of money, just like the top movie stars or famous fashion designers.

But **you don't need to buy anything**. Simply leaf through the book and admire each carefully crafted object. Imagine: they could have been designed in a thousand different ways. **The designer's imagination knows no bounds.**

This book will introduce you to the **designers** who have created the chosen objects. **Each object is introduced by two names**. The first has been invented just for this book. The second, in small print, is the original name given by the designer. **Special icons** will tell you when an object was designed, what material it is made of, and what functions it can perform. You will also learn the name of the company producing it. **All the objects are listed in two ways**: by their picture in the diagram at the beginning of the book; and under their name (invented and original) in the index at the end.

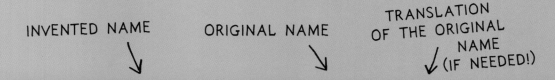

INVENTED NAME ↓   ORIGINAL NAME ↓   TRANSLATION OF THE ORIGINAL NAME (IF NEEDED!) ↓

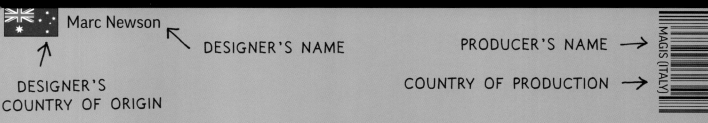

coral reef drainer DISH DOCTOR (DISH DOCTOR)

Marc Newson ← DESIGNER'S NAME   PRODUCER'S NAME →   MAGIS (ITALY)

↑ DESIGNER'S COUNTRY OF ORIGIN   COUNTRY OF PRODUCTION →

WHAT MATERIAL IT IS MADE OF ↓

WHEN THE OBJECT WAS DESIGNED →   1997   WHAT FUNCTION IT CAN PERFORM ←

contents

key

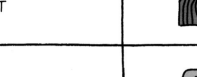 DATE THE OBJECT WAS DESIGNED

OBJECT MADE OF WOOD

OBJECT MADE OF METAL

 OBJECT MADE OF PAPER

OBJECT MADE OF GLASS

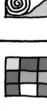 OBJECT MADE OF FABRIC

OBJECT MADE OF STRAW

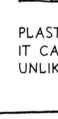 OBJECT MADE OF PLASTIC

PLASTIC IS A MAN-MADE MATERIAL. IT CAN'T BE FOUND IN NATURE, UNLIKE WOOD OR STONE.

 OBJECT MADE OF WIRE

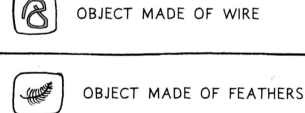 OBJECT MADE OF FEATHERS

 OBJECT MADE OF ROPE

 OBJECT MADE OF PLASTER

 OBJECT MADE OF LEATHER

OBJECT MADE OF PORCELAIN

 OBJECT MADE OF STONE

THE DESIGNER'S HOME COUNTRY

BELGIUM

UNITED KINGDOM

NETHERLANDS

HUNGARY

IRELAND

SWITZERLAND

FRANCE

FINLAND

USA

JAPAN

ITALY

DENMARK

SWEDEN

CANADA

BRAZIL

AUSTRALIA

EGYPT

POLAND

SPAIN

INDIA

ISRAEL

GERMANY

	FOR SITTING ON		FOR LYING ON		FOR SLEEPING ON
	FOR PLAYING WITH		FOR WASHING WITH		ACCESSORIES, OR SMALL YET HUGELY USEFUL THINGS
	LIGHTING		STORAGE		DECORATION

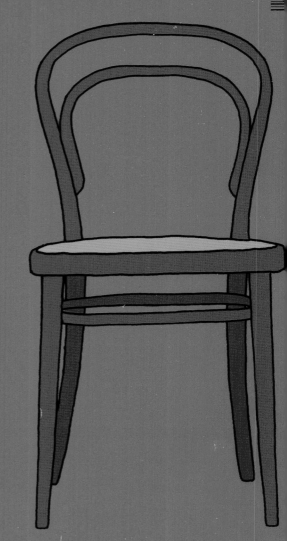

Michael Thonet

Here's **the most famous chair ever made**. Ask your parents or grandparents – no doubt they will recognize it. They might still have one at home. Michael Thonet designed it over 150 years ago. It's called 'the chair of chairs' – for many reasons.

First, it was so much cheaper than other chairs that **everyone could afford it**. That's because it was the **first mass-produced chair** – it was made in big factories, not in small workshops. Second, it consisted of only six parts and several screws, so it could be **easily assembled** in a shop, rather than in a factory. Third, its simple construction allowed **simple packaging**, in boxes one metre square. Fourth, it was **easy and cheap to transport** all over the world. It soon became popular not only in Europe, but also in North and South America, Asia and Africa.

Last, but not least: it was, and still is, a very elegant and enduring chair. No wonder it has **sold over 50 million copies**. No other piece of furniture can boast such sales.

Most importantly, Thonet's chair is still produced.

HOW CHAIRS WERE
PACKED

HOW TO ASSEMBLE
THE SIMPLE PARTS

1859

CHARLIE CHAPLIN
ON THONET'S
CHAIR

MICHAEL THONET

015

Charles Rennie Mackintosh

CASSINA (ITALY)

What's the **purpose of a chair**? It's for sitting on, surely. A hundred years ago everyone thought so. Well, almost everyone. The designer Charles Rennie Mackintosh had **a different idea**.

Once, Mackintosh was designing a house on a hill. For one of its bedrooms, he created a huge bed and very tall wardrobes, but he felt there was still something missing. Finally, it occurred to him that there should be a chair in the room. Not for sitting, but **to help compose a beautiful and harmonious whole**.

Mackintosh's chair is not particularly comfortable - but it does have presence. It has a very, very tall back which **resembles a ladder**, finished off with a decorative grating – ideal for drying socks, except it is too important for that. It's the first chair whose appearance matters more than its purpose.

CHARLES RENNIE MACKINTOSH

CHARLES'S WIFE, MARGARET
MACDONALD MACKINTOSH,
. ALSO AN ARTIST — SHE WAS
A PAINTER AND DESIGNER.

1903

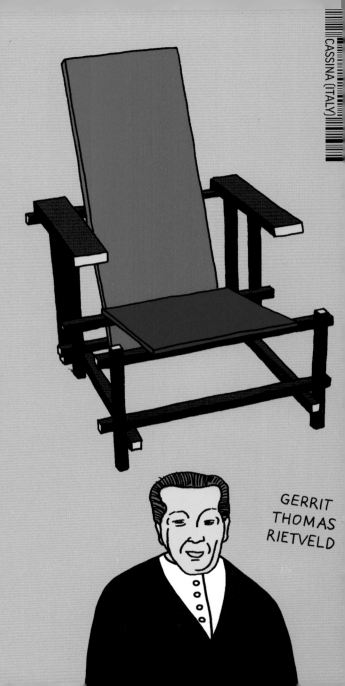

Before we can discuss the **Red and Blue Chair**, we need to look at **Piet Mondrian's paintings**. They're all about straight lines: horizontal and vertical. That's because Mondrian painted with the help of his ruler and set square. He chose only three colours: **blue, red and yellow**. (He also used white, black and grey, but he called them 'non-colours'.)

The original chair was in plain wood. But the designer, Rietveld, happened to be Mondrian's friend and liked these three-colour works, so he decided to paint his chair in a similar way.

The chair is **hard and not very comfortable** – certainly not the kind of armchair in which your dad can nod off while reading his book. And that's the whole point – Rietveld wanted his chair to **keep people alert and aware**, not drowsy and droopy.

GERRIT THOMAS RIETVELD

PIET MONDRIAN'S
PAINTINGS

1918

019

The best ideas can spring from unusual circumstances. For instance, Marcel Breuer was **riding his bike** when he suddenly thought: If a steel tube can be bent to make a handlebar, surely it can be bent to make an armchair?

And he was right: **steel tubing** has every advantage. It's cheap, easy to produce, hygienic, and – most importantly – springy, so it can be used instead of springs. To produce his armchair, Breuer turned to a bicycle factory for help. The result surpassed his expectations. Soon other designers started to use steel tubing, too.

And that's how **one bike ride changed furniture design forever**.

But why is the chair called Wassily? One of Breuer's friends admired the armchair so much that he was given an early specimen. And because this friend happened to be the famous Russian painter **Wassily Kandinsky**, the armchair was named after him. Before that, it was simply called B3.

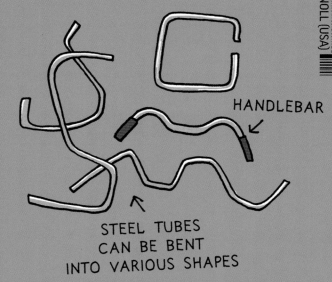

HANDLEBAR

STEEL TUBES CAN BE BENT INTO VARIOUS SHAPES

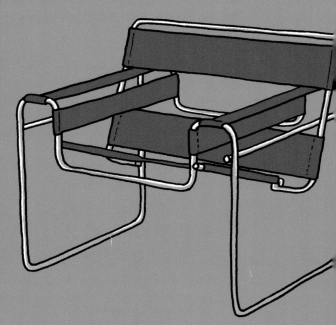

KNOLL (USA)

Eileen Gray

If you like **eating in bed**, then this clever little table is for you. Eileen Gray designed it for her sister, who loved having breakfast-in-bed.

You can place the top of this one-legged table directly above your bed, then make it higher or lower to suit you and your pillows. And you can easily wipe away strawberry jam or scrambled eggs, because it's made of **steel tubes and glass**.

Eileen Gray invented the name **E1027** for the summer house she was building for herself and her fiancé, Jean Badovici. The bedside table was supposed to go in one of the guest rooms, so it was also called E1027. But what does that name mean? If you enjoy code-cracking, you may have guessed that it's **a secret code**. **E** stands for Eileen, and the numbers stand for letters of the alphabet: **10** means **J**, as in Jean; **2** means **B**, as in Badovici; and **7** means **G**, as in Gray. Clever, isn't it?

EILEEN GRAY

THE HEIGHT OF THE TABLE CAN BE ADJUSTED

 Le Corbusier ✚ Pierre Jeanneret ▮ Charlotte Perriand

Le Corbusier argued that a house was a machine for sleeping in. To him, pieces of furniture were also **machines**, each with its specific purpose and function. He decided to design three new armchairs, each with a different use.

The **armchair for relaxing** is all soft leather cushions – you can sink into it and unwind. The **armchair for conversing** has very narrow arms, so you can't sprawl in it – you have to sit straight and listen to every word. But the most unusual design is the **LC4 – a cross between a bed and an armchair**. It resembles the 'chaise longue' designed in the eighteenth-century: a reclining chair with a seat so long that you could rest your legs.

Le Corbusier's version of this long chair is far better than its predecessors. It perfectly adjusts to the human body and **can accommodate any position**. LC4 was produced in the workshop run by Le Corbusier (hence LC) and his cousin Pierre Jeanneret, but it was thought out mainly by a young designer, Charlotte Perriand. Because all three cooperated on each project, all three signed each design.

THE ARMCHAIR
FOR RELAXING

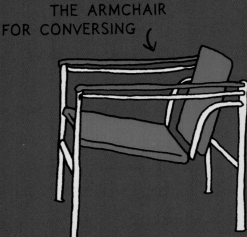

THE ARMCHAIR
FOR CONVERSING

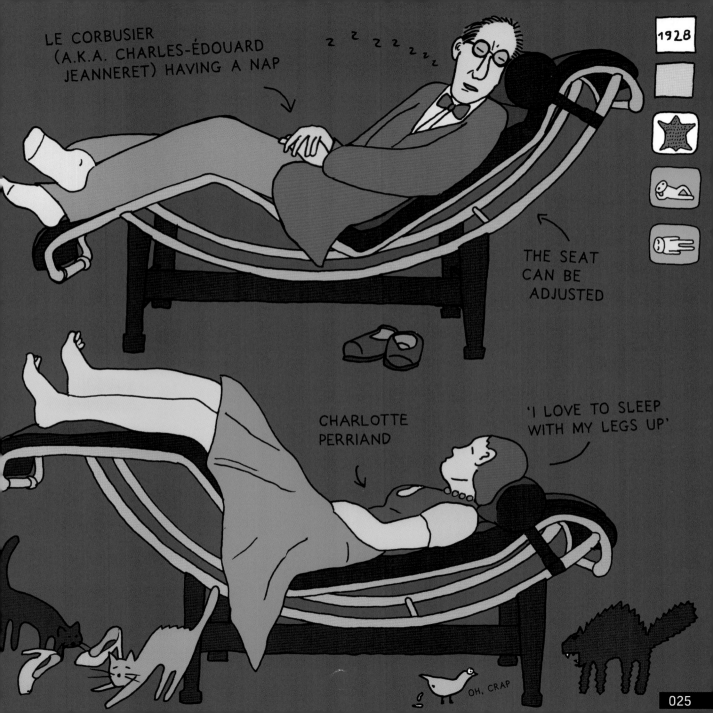

PHARAOH

THE ANCIENT
THRONE OF
THE PHARAOH

KNOLL (USA)

In 1929, the **Spanish king** was to sit in the German Pavilion to oversee the opening ceremony of **the Barcelona International Exhibition**. A **very important chair** was called for. The king was full of majesty, the building was full of modernity, and the chair had to match the **grand occasion**.

Ludwig Mies van der Rohe, the designer of both pavilion and chair, had a hard nut to crack – **a modern throne**? Traditionally, thrones are wooden, with high backs, decorated with heavy fabric and golden crowns. Not exactly a modern project, or a thrilling prospect for a modern designer. So he searched and searched until he finally found a royal chair with a difference: **an ancient throne for pharaohs and Greek kings**. It looked like a folding chair, but the X created by its legs symbolized power, according to Egyptian beliefs. Ludwig Mies van der Rohe was relieved. That was exactly the inspiration he was looking for.

His special armchair soon gained the reputation of **'a design worthy of kings'**.

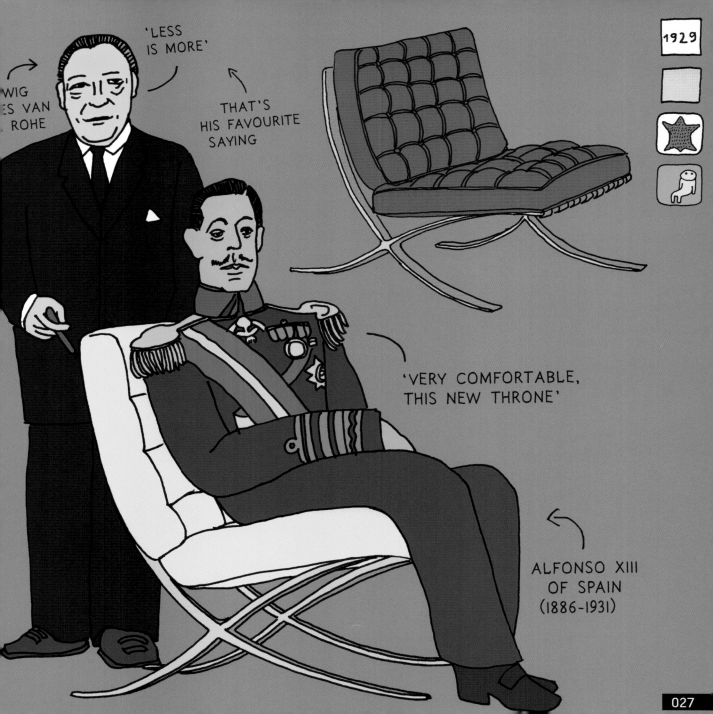

Alvar Aalto

Any idea what Eskimo leather breeches or Finnish fjords look like? No? What about a puddle? An ordinary puddle, together with the trousers and the fjords, helped the designer Alvar Aalto to think up his new vase. He almost named it Eskimonaisen nahkahousut, which in Finnish means **'the leather trousers of a young Sami girl'.** He didn't call it **Finland**, though the vase won a competition to be the national symbol. He didn't call it **Puddle**, though he used this nickname to speak about his vase. He simply named it 'Savoy' after the Savoy Restaurant in Helsinki, which he also created. The first specimens of his new design decorated this luxurious place.

One more important detail: Aalto never referred to his object as a vase. He thought that buyers would know best what it was and the purpose it may serve.

A HAVEN
FOR YOUR FISH

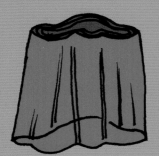

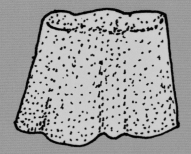

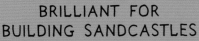

BRILLIANT FOR
BUILDING SANDCASTLES

STORES YOUR BRUSHES
AND CRAYONS

● Isamu Noguchi

Isamu Noguchi was first and foremost a sculptor, so his pieces of furniture look like sculptures. Have a look at this famous **coffee table: two identical pieces of wood and a glass top**. Noguchi designed it for the director of the Museum of Modern Art in New York. Naturally, the director liked it. It might be the most beautiful coffee table in the world: **a piece of furniture and a work of art in one**.

HERMAN MILLER (USA), VITRA (SWITZERLAND)

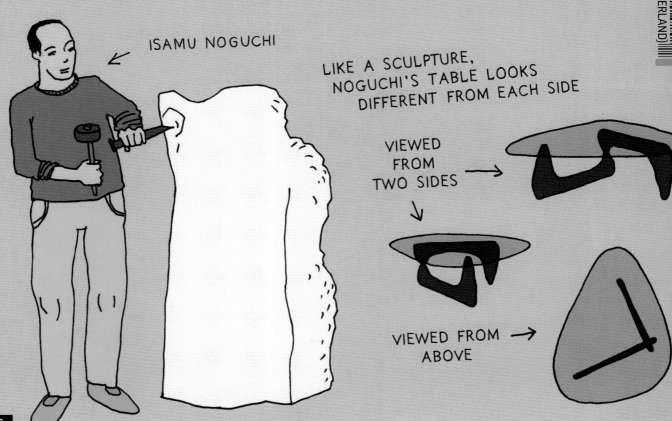

ISAMU NOGUCHI

LIKE A SCULPTURE, NOGUCHI'S TABLE LOOKS DIFFERENT FROM EACH SIDE

VIEWED FROM TWO SIDES →

VIEWED FROM ABOVE →

Charles and Ray Eames

Husband and wife, Charles and Ray Eames constructed a machine for **moulding plywood into different shapes**, which helped them make elegant and comfortable chairs ... as well as a **plywood elephant**. This toy was so difficult and expensive to produce that originally only two were made.

The elephant then had to wait for a very long time, but finally in 2007, the Swiss company Vitra prepared a special limited edition of **one thousand elephants** to celebrate the hundredth birthday of Charles Eames. They were still very expensive, so the only people who could afford them were rich collectors, rather than ordinary parents who might love to buy one for their children.

But the Eames had designed the elephant **especially for children**! So Vitra spent two more years figuring out how to produce cheaper elephants made of plastic. They look exactly like their plywood cousins, but they cost less and are more durable. Charles and Ray Eames would have been happy. They wanted their furniture to be owned by as many people as possible.

CHARLES EAMES

RAY EAMES

Carlo Mollino

Carlo Mollino was an extremely active person with numerous interests and hobbies. He was a photographer, writer and architect; he designed clothes, furniture and interiors. He also enjoyed sports: **flying aeroplanes** (crazy acrobatic manoeuvres brought him pure joy), **skiing** and **racing cars**. He even designed planes and racing cars himself. It's surprising that he found time for all these activities, but he claimed they had a lot in common.

What do Mollino's designs have in common with skiing? Or with flying aeroplanes? Have a look at this table. When Carlo Mollino invented its 'legs', he was thinking of the tracks that planes and skis leave behind. There are **no acute angles**, because sudden sharp turns are impossible when you ski or fly a plane. The table is made of bent and cut-out plywood, and has a glass top.

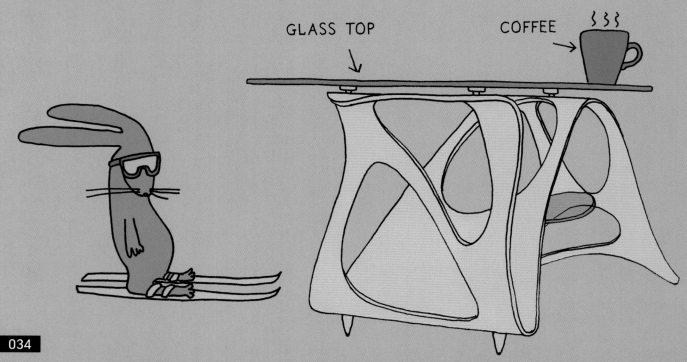

GLASS TOP

COFFEE

CARLO
MOLLINO

Jean Prouvé

Designers who consider themselves artists often concentrate first on what their piece of furniture should look like – how to make it can be worked out later. But a designer who is an engineer and architect, like Jean Prouvé, starts with the **material and construction** for a new piece of furniture.

The appearance of this table was determined by its unusual construction: **slanted legs**. Prouvé carefully observed **bridges** and **flyovers**. As a metal smith, he favoured **steel** for the legs. The table was commissioned by the French government to go in houses that were built specially for French people living in Africa. But French clerks didn't like the steel house designed by Prouvé; it also turned out to be too expensive, so only three were built. The table was luckier – it has been in production ever since.

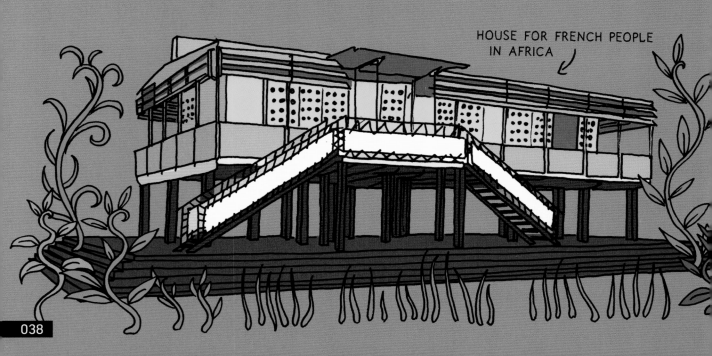

HOUSE FOR FRENCH PEOPLE IN AFRICA

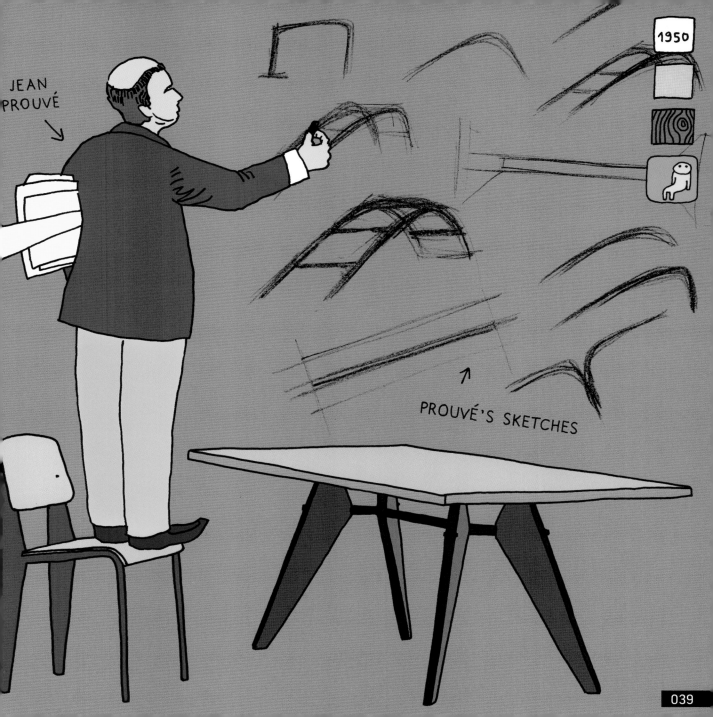

JEAN PROUVÉ

1950

PROUVÉ'S SKETCHES

039

FRITZ HANSEN (DENMARK)

Arne Jacobsen

Before Arne Jacobsen started to design his chair, he asked himself: **what kind of chair do people need**? In his opinion, an ideal chair had to be: 1. **small** – for a small kitchen; 2. **light** and easy to move; and 3. **cheap**. Jacobsen's chair is stackable, too; you can pile several up in a tiny kitchen.

Look at its shape. It's a bit like **an ant with its head raised**. That's why the chair is called 'myren' (the ant) in Danish. Jacobsen gave it **three legs**, one front and two back. But his bosses claimed nobody would buy a three-legged chair, so they refused to produce it. Jacobsen was so sure he was right that he offered to buy all the chairs back if they didn't sell. Luckily, as you may have guessed, he didn't have to do that – the ant chair proved very popular.

A four-legged version for disbelievers also went into production, but only after Jacobsen's death.

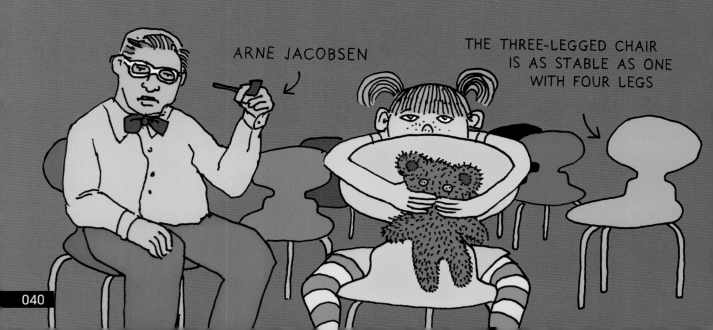

ARNE JACOBSEN

THE THREE-LEGGED CHAIR IS AS STABLE AS ONE WITH FOUR LEGS

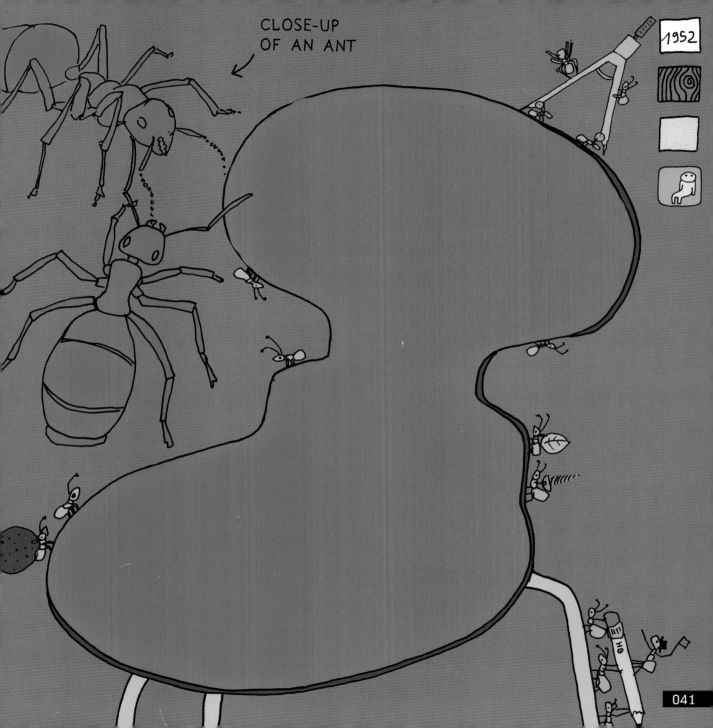

KNOLL (USA)

Harry Bertoia

One of the many things to consider when designing an object is the **material**. Will the finished product be light or heavy? Solid or fragile? What shape will it be? That all depends on the material used for its construction. An excellent idea for the material often means an **excellent idea** for the design.

Do you remember Breuer's armchair made of bike tubes?* Harry Bertoia went one better when he invented a chair of **steel mesh**, which is **extremely light** and can be **easily bent** into shape. Best of all, it's **hardly visible**, so when you sit in Bertoia's chair, you feel like a magician miraculously floating above the ground. What else would you expect of the chair **made of air**!

A MAGICIAN

HARRY BERTOIA

*IF NOT, CHECK PAGE 20

1952

043

HERMAN MILLER (USA), VITRA (SWITZERLAND)

George Nelson

Do you think the **coconut** was George Nelson's **favourite fruit**? Probably, given the shape of his famous armchair. Nelson divided the coconut into eight equal segments, then placed one of them onto a steel frame – and his design was ready! He made the outside **white, like coconut flesh**, and the inside **brown, like the shell**. The coconut armchair is also very comfortable, because its seat can be fixed in different positions.

EXAMPLES
OF NELSON'S OTHER
FAMOUS DESIGNS

THE PALM CRAB
IS AN EXPERT
AT CRACKING
COCONUTS

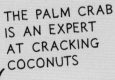

COCONUT

THE BIGGEST
ARTHROPOD
IN THE WORLD

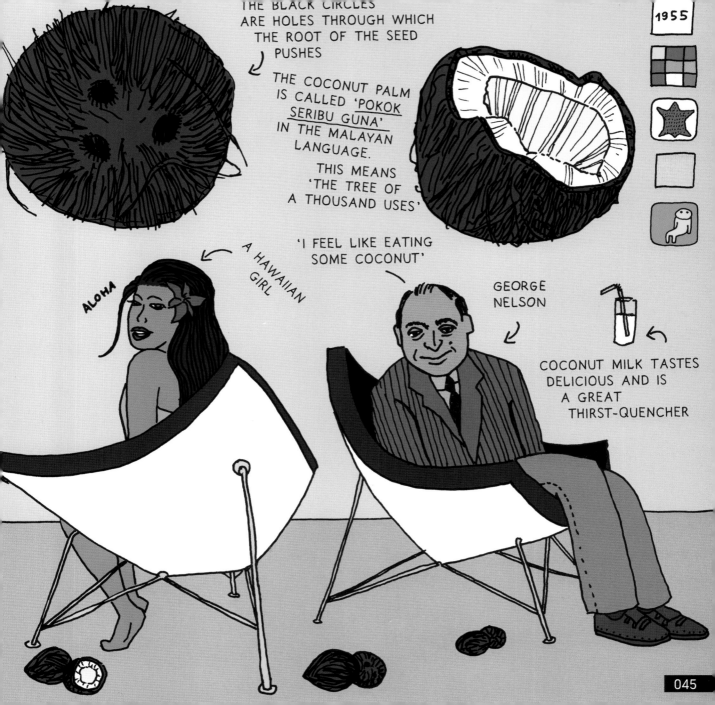

KNOLL (USA)

Eero Saarinen

Eero Saarinen noticed that the dining room of a typical American family was a forest of legs – four legs on a table, four chairs with four legs each ... not to mention the human legs. That's way **too many legs** in one room – it looks **ugly and messy**. So Saarinen decided to fix that. He designed a chair and a table that each stand on one leg only. He called them **Tulip**, though they look **more like wine glasses** than flowers.

'LOOK AT ALL THESE LEGS!'

Achille and Pier Giacomo Castiglioni

The Castiglioni brothers observed that lights tend to hang from the middle of the ceiling. If you want your table well-lit, you must place it under the light, right in the middle of the room. Or you have to rip up the ceiling to move the light, which is tricky and could be dangerous. If you then decide to shift the table a little to the left, or put it by the window, you have to make a hole in the ceiling again!

The brothers thought, and thought, and thought. In the end, they looked out the window and saw **a street lamp**. It stood on the pavement, but lit the street as well. That is how they invented the **Arco lamp**. 'Arco' means '**arch**' in Italian: thanks to its arch, the lamp can stand on the floor and light the centre of the table. To keep it from toppling, it has a **heavy marble base**. It weighs around **65 kilograms** – the weight of three small boys or one medium-sized man.

'SOMETHING LIKE A STREET LAMP?'

'THAT'S IT!'

ACHILLE CASTIGLIONI

PIER GIACOMO CASTIGLIONI

049

Eero Aarnio

One day, Eero Aarnio decided that he would like a **unique armchair**. He started to draw unusual and bizarre shapes. But after many trials, he settled on a **simple sphere**. He drew a circle the size he wanted his armchair to be (so the scale of his model was 1:1). Then he pinned his drawing to the wall and pretended to sit in it. But his head was sticking out, so he called his wife and asked her to draw around his head. At that stage he knew how big the armchair should be. Once he'd checked that a sphere of that size could squeeze through the door, the design was ready. Soon, he could actually sit in his armchair.

Aarnio called it **a room inside a room**, because it's very cosy inside. He even installed a telephone in his!

YOU CAN HAVE A PHONE INSIDE

PURRRR

A CAT TOY

Franco Teodoro, Cesare Paolini, Piero Gatti

Franco Teodoro, Cesare Paolini and Piero Gatti wanted to create **a super-comfortable armchair.** One where you could sit, lie or sprawl, whichever way you wanted. One that would perfectly mould not only to your body, but anybody's body.

Sounds great, but how to go about it? The designers thought of the imprint a body leaves in soft snow. They thought of how water flows around a body. Was there a **material that could imitate snow or water?** How about those rustic mattresses filled with leaves or hay? The problem with these was that they soon become hard and uncomfortable. How about glass balls, rubber balls, ping-pong balls … small objects that would move when you sat on them? Unfortunately, everything they thought of was too expensive or too heavy, or both.

Luckily for us, the designers discovered the material used on construction sites: polystyrene pellets, similar to tiny Styrofoam balls. **Light, cheap, and ideal.** So they sewed up **a sack**, filled it with tiny balls – and it worked!

CESARE PAOLINI

ZANOTTA (ITALY)

PIERO
GATTI

FRANCO
EODORO

1968

053

Gaetano Pesce

Usually a piece of furniture is a practical object. But occasionally it will convey **an important message** from its designer, in this case Gaetano Pesce.

Pesce thought that **women worked too hard**, taking care of the house, children, dogs, cats, husbands... He thought they were slogging away **like prisoners**. He created an armchair that looked like **a woman chained to a ball**, to symbolize the shackles of women's everyday chores. Pesce now laughs that his idea has not been very successful, because his message is often misread. People imagine that the ball is a child, while the armchair represents motherly love.

But what about the armchair's puzzling name: Up 5 | Up 6? When Pesce saw how coffee was **vacuum-packed**, he wanted his armchair packed in the same way. He had it put into a plastic bag, and the air was sucked out until the parcel was flat as a pancake. When the new owner cut the plastic bag, air flowed in, and the foam armchair **recovered its full feminine shape**. The air filled the chair 'up'! Today the armchair is no longer packed this way, but the name has remained.

PRISONER WITH A BALL AND CHAIN

PRISONERS HAVE TO WEAR STRIPY UNIFORMS TO BE OBVIOUS

HEAVY BALL

GAETANO PESCE

B&B ITALIA (ITALY)

VVZZZMMMM

1969

055

Verner Panton

Vernon Panton noticed that many people decorate their homes as if they were afraid of lively, cheerful colours. Their homes look rather sad with dark brown furniture, light brown floors and carpets, beige throws and curtains. Now and then, someone may boldly add another colour – but it's so pale that no one can spot it.

Panton decided he would challenge this brown dreariness by introducing **lively colours that encouraged joy and smiles**. He was a cheerful person who enjoyed a good laugh, and he used to say, 'Sitting is great fun!' His colourful chairs, armchairs, and sofas are joyous and playful – like his famous plastic chair that is named after its designer: Panton. Or Heart Cone, a heart-shaped armchair. Panton's strangest design is his **Living Tower** sofa. With four levels, **it looks like a climbing frame**. You can use it any way you wish.

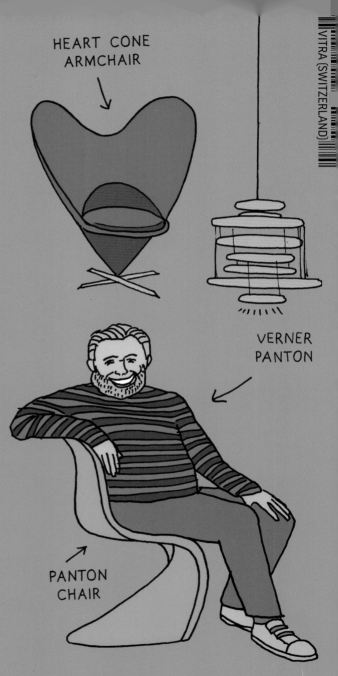

HEART CONE ARMCHAIR

VERNER PANTON

PANTON CHAIR

Studio 65 (Franco Audrito and the Team)

GUFRAM (ITALY), HELLER (USA)

In 1933, the famous painter **Salvador Dalí** created the artwork, 'Face of Mae West Which Can Be Used as an Apartment'. Look carefully at the woman in Dalí's strange surreal portrait: her hair resembles curtains, her eyes are paintings on the wall, her nose is a fireplace, and **a sofa forms her lips**. This lip sofa really exists, because Dalí made it soon after he made his painting.

Almost forty years later, the architects from Studio 65 took his idea further and designed Sofa Bocca. Both the sofas are shaped like lips, yet they seem to differ. Why? The answer is simple. Over the forty years, the ideal of female beauty had changed; so did **the ideal shape of lips**. Salvador Dalí was inspired by the lips of **the 1930s Hollywood star, Mae West**. The Studio 65 team took their inspiration from the beauty of their times, **Marilyn Monroe**. (Be careful if you sit on this sofa – you might be gobbled up!)

SALVADOR DALÍ'S PAINTING: 'FACE OF MAE WEST WHICH CAN BE USED AS AN APARTMENT'

SALVADOR DALÍ

MAE WEST

DALÍ'S LIP SOFA

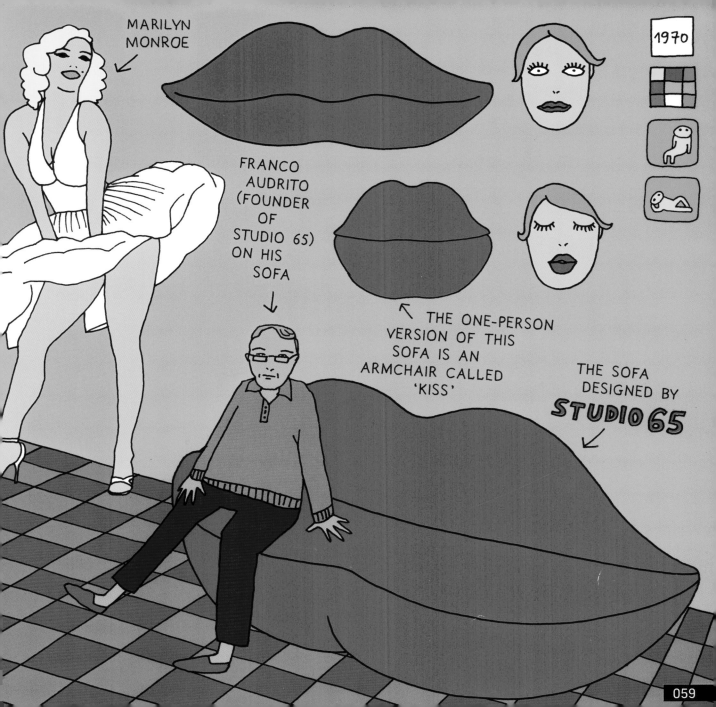

MARILYN MONROE

FRANCO AUDRITO (FOUNDER OF STUDIO 65) ON HIS SOFA

THE ONE-PERSON VERSION OF THIS SOFA IS AN ARMCHAIR CALLED 'KISS'

THE SOFA DESIGNED BY STUDIO 65

1970

DONATO D'URBINO

GIONATAN DE PAS

PAOLO LOMAZZI

POLTRONOVA (ITALY)

In design, anything is possible. If a sofa can turn up as Marilyn Monroe's lips, why not as **a giant baseball glove**?

This huge mitt was created to celebrate **the legend of American baseball – Joe DiMaggio**. He won fame and popularity, and became an American national hero. But he never forgot that his family had come to the United States from Italy, so three Italian designers – Jonathan De Pas, Donato D'Urbino, Paolo Lomazzi – erected this **amusing armchair monument** to DiMaggio. They must have been big baseball fans! They didn't mind that most people couldn't imagine a baseball glove as an armchair. That was the whole point. Being creative in design often means breaking the rules.

GUFRAM (ITALY)

Sturm Group (Giorgio Ceretti, Pietro Derossi and Riccardo Rosso)

If you have read **_Alice in Wonderland_**, do you remember how Alice grew enormous or very, very tiny whenever she ate or drank? If you get the chance to sit on this sofa, you'll **feel just like Alice**. It makes you wonder, 'have I drunk something that's turned me into a little gnome? Or has the grass gobbled up something to make it so tall?' You don't often stumble upon **towering clumps of grass**. Such wonderful sofas are equally rare. The designers of this one wanted to **feel as if they were lying in a meadow**. Literally.

← ENORMOUS ALICE

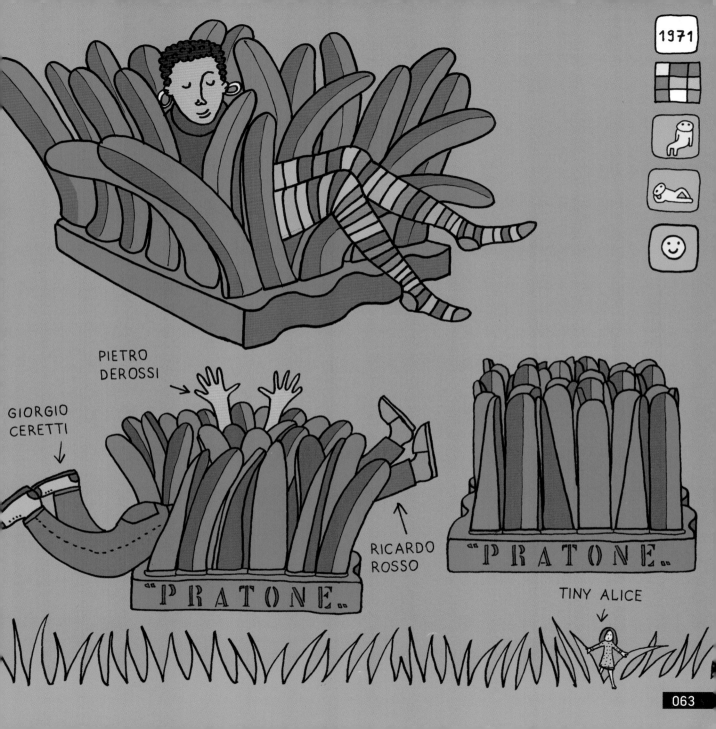

PIETRO
DEROSSI

GIORGIO
CERETTI

RICARDO
ROSSO

"PRATONE"

"PRATONE"

TINY ALICE

1971

IKEA Team

A very important **IKEA** designer came home one day and saw to his horror that his expensive sofa was no longer white and pristine. It was damaged and filthy.

The man was devastated. He called his wife, children, and dog, and demanded an answer: who did it? Well, it soon became clear that the sofa was the Wild West, and that Indians were involved, which included the dog that had failed to warn them about the cowboys...

The man was furious, but he didn't shout at his children (because it's not allowed in **Sweden**). Instead, he started imagining a **sofa that could survive children**. Solid enough to jump on. Soft enough that you wouldn't crack your head on it. With a cover that was easy to take off and wash. And so cheap that everyone could buy it.

That's how the **Klippan sofa** was invented. Especially for children.

'IT HAS TO SURVIVE ALL THE JUMPING'

'AND SLEEPING'

'AND PIZZA-EATING'

'AND PLAYING WITH CRAYONS AND PLASTICINE'

At first glance, this object looks like **a boxing ring**. But what about the Japanese mats, and the corner lamps? In fact, **no one fights here**. The Japanese designer Masanori Umeda outlined the functions of this strange piece of furniture:

1. You can **sleep and rest** on it. (Japanese beds are low and firm.)

2. You can sit in the middle, cross your legs and **meditate**, that is, try to calm down and get rid of useless thoughts.

3. It can be used as a small lounge where you invite your friends to sit together on the mats and enjoy a friendly **conversation** over cups of fragrant tea.

4. It makes a great **playpen** for children and adults. You feel safe in it, because Tawaraya is soft and pliant, with rubber cords to keep you from falling out. Here you can jump, run, exercise – or practise boxing...

IS NO LONGER PRODUCED

ONLY 100 SPECIMENS WERE MADE

* CONSUMER - SOMEONE WHO BUYS OR USES SOMETHING

Once, Frank Schreiner took his mother to a shop with furniture made by famous designers. When she saw some **wire-mesh chairs**, she told him they reminded her of **shopping trolleys**.** Probably, she wasn't very impressed. But Schreiner was delighted. Instantly, he knew what he was going to do with the old shopping trolley he used as a washing basket.

By transforming it into a chair, he was **poking fun at the way we pay a fortune for famous designs**. The trolley chair wasn't meant to be mass-produced – it was created as a **work of art**.

** THE SHOPPING TROLLEY WAS INVENTED IN 1936 BY SYLVAN GOLDMAN, WHO ADAPTED A FOLDING CHAIR HE'D DESIGNED, AND ATTACHED WIRE BASKETS AND WHEELS.

A WIRE-MESH CHAIR DISLIKED BY FRANK SCHREINER'S MUM

FANCY THIS TROLLEY CHAIR?

FRANK SCHREINER

MODEL WITH WHEELS

Michele De Lucchi

'If a lamp works on the moon, it'll work anywhere,' thought Michele De Lucchi, and he went on to create Tolomeo – **a lamp fit for a lunar vehicle**. Its stem resembles a **robotic arm**, which can be bent any way you want, to light whatever you want. Space technology must be **reliable**, so De Lucchi used aluminium, which is also **very lightweight**. To make the lamp even lighter he left its mechanism exposed, without a cover. He wasn't trying to make it pretty. Why would you need attractive objects in space?

THE MOON

MICHELE DE LUCCHI

THE LAMP WAS NAMED AFTER THE ANCIENT GREEK ASTRONOMER, PTOLEMY

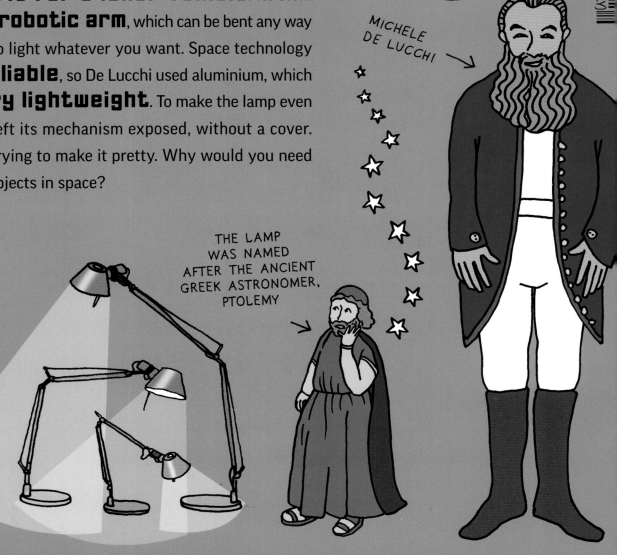

ARTEMIDE (ITALY)

Philippe Starck

Philippe Starck is the brightest star among designers – for two reasons. First, he's extremely hard-working and versatile. **He can design almost anything**, just like that: furniture, lamps, forks, clothes, glasses, shoes, suitcases, kettles, taps, motorcycles, yachts, cars, gas masks, toys, toothbrushes. Even pasta!

Second, he doesn't invent ordinary things. **He wants to surprise**. For instance, he's invented a lamp that looks like a machine gun, a stool resembling a tooth, and a chair that's a wheelbarrow. He also designed **the world-famous citrus squeezer** – a far cry from the usual.

PHILIPPE S+ARCK

LEMON

THE CHE

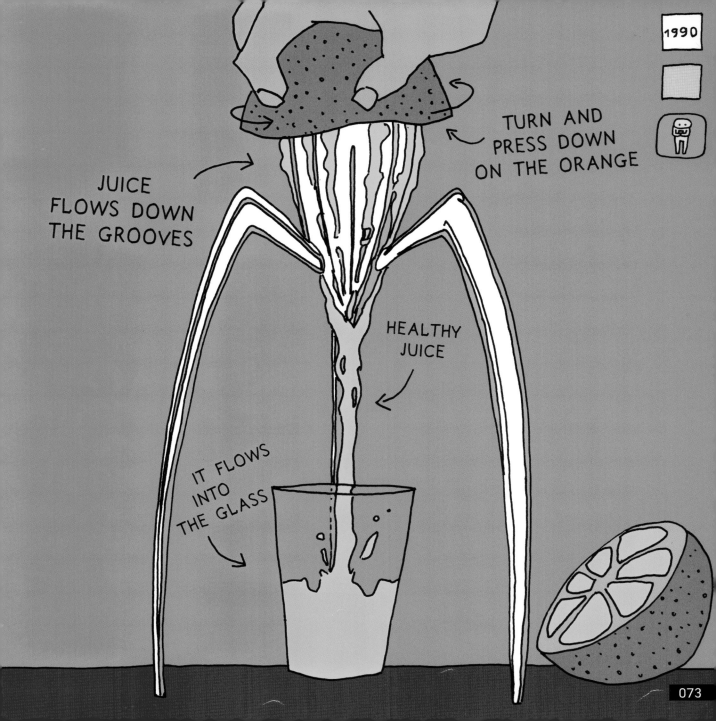

Starck had been in a restaurant eating delicious seafood, when he looked at the octopus on his plate, then at the lemon in his hand. He wiped his mouth with a napkin and – presto! – on the greasy napkin he drew the squeezer. He immediately rushed out and showed the napkin to the owner of the Alessi company.

Is the squeezer **an octopus, or a spaceship on spindly legs**?

A MILITARISTIC NEIGHBOUR SHOOTS FROM STARCK'S MACHINE-GUN LAMP

DROOG DESIGN (HOLLAND)

Think of the **masses of things thrown out** that end up in skips, then in dumps. We keep buying new objects, even when the old ones aren't very old. They're **not exactly garbage**, either. Tejo Remy thought that people were mad, always chasing after newer things. 'I protest!' he cried, and invented a new object made entirely out of old things. It's **creative recycling**. He collected drawers from discarded chests and built a box for each one. Then, he arranged all the boxes into a fantastic pile and tied the whole lot together with rope. The result was amazing: **a unique, modern design**. Remy's recycled chest of drawers reminds us that old things have their own intriguing past that we should respect.

A LAMP MADE FROM AN OLD BOTTLE

TIE OLD THINGS WITH ROPE TO CREATE AN EXTRAORDINARY PIECE OF FURNITURE

TEJO REMY

ROPE'S NOT JUST FOR TY[ING] DRAWERS — HERE'S AN ARMC[HAIR] DESIGNED BY REMY, MADE OF OLD RAGS

EACH DRAWER ONCE BELONGED TO A DIFFERENT CHEST

1991

THE DRAWERS ARE TIED TOGETHER WITH A JUTE ROPE

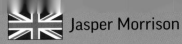 Jasper Morrison

Jasper Morrison believes that a well-designed object should be **plain and simple**, without fancy decorations or frills. All his designs are as straightforward as possible. When designing a **bird feeder**, he limited himself to the most essential elements. First of all, a space for food: **a plate** would be good, deep enough for seeds to stay inside. Second, a roof to protect the food from rain and snow: **another plate** would do, bigger than the first, and turned upside down. Third, something to hang the feeder with: **a coat-hanger wire** that could join the two plates. With a length of wire left underneath, the feeder can be stuck in the ground. **As simple as that!**

JASPER MORRISON

1991

079

punnet chair

 Frank Gehry

The famous Frank Gehry designs unusual buildings which swirl, wriggle and roll – more like sculptures than architectural constructions.

Like most good architects, he can see at a glance how a thing has been made. Once, in Poland, he spotted **a fruit punnet**. He loved the way the **ribbons of wood were woven together**. This gave him the idea of **weaving an armchair** himself. Well, it wasn't as simple as he thought. But Gehry is a stubborn guy. He worked on his design for more than three years and tried over 120 models, until at last he succeeded. Instead of the pine wood shavings that make a punnet, he used extra-thin and flexible **white maple veneers**, moulded into shape while still wet. But you must admit, the resemblance is striking.

Gehry named his armchair **Power Play**, because hockey is his passion. He comes from **Canada, home of hockey** (and maple syrup). In hockey, 'power play' is when one team outnumbers the other.

KNOLL (USA)

PUNNETS FILLED
WITH DELICIOUS
FRUIT

FRANK GEHRY'S
UNUSUAL BUILDINGS

1991

FRANK GEHRY →

POWER PLAY
ARMCHAIR

9

THE CAMPANA BROTHERS' STUDY

EDRA (ITALY)

Why do designers design what they do? Sometimes their ideas are shaped by the place where they grew up. Humberto and Fernando Campana live in **São Paolo, Brazil**. This city has many **favelas**, or very poor **shanty towns**. The residents **build their shacks from what they can find in the streets**: scrap metal, bits of wood, rubber tyres, wires, ropes and other junk. The Campana brothers use the same method – their design is born in the street. At the start of their career they didn't have much money, so they scavenged whatever they could to make furniture. The garage that served as their studio looked like a crazy collector's lab. These days, the brothers are world-famous and rich, but they still use **scrap materials**. They say that their unpredictable pieces are **inspired by the chaos and beauty of the city** they live in.

VERMELHA (RED)

FERNANDO CAMPANA

AN ARMCHA
MADE FROM
500 METRE:
OF SPECIAL
ROPE. THE FI
MODEL USE
CORD BOUG
FROM A STRE
STALL IN
SÃO PAOL(

1993

2004

HUMBERTO CAMPANA

CORALLO (CORAL)

THIS CORAL-PINK WIRE CHAIR RESEMBLES A SPRAWLING REEF OFF THE COAST OF BRAZIL

AN ARMCHAIR FROM PIECES
OF WOOD FOUND IN THE STREET,
CONSTRUCTED LIKE THE SHACKS
IN BRAZILIAN SHANTY TOWNS

1991

FAVELA

MULTIDÃO
(CROWD)

2002

A CHAIR MADE OUT OF TRADITIONAL
COTTON DOLLS FROM NORTH-EASTERN BRAZIL

2007

AN ARMCHAIR WHERE ALLIGATORS
AND SNAKES SLOUGH THEIR SKINS

LEATHERWORKS

Alessandro Mendini

Have you ever been in love? If so, you know what it means: your sweetheart is always on your mind, no matter what. This happened to Alessandro Mendini. **He was madly in love** when he was asked to design a corkscrew. He drew many different designs, but ... no matter what he did, **each corkscrew looked like his fiancée**! Finally, he gave in. He deliberately drew a corkscrew with the **silhouette and face of a beautiful girl**. Thus, **Anna G.** was created.

Ten years later, Mendini drew another corkscrew – **his self-portrait**. Now the girl had a boyfriend. **Alessandro M.** takes on numerous guises: a cook, a king, even a ghost.

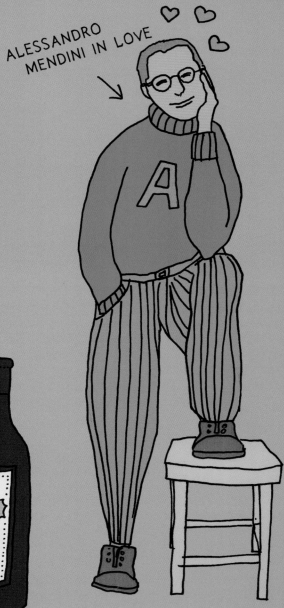

ALESSANDRO
MENDINI IN LOVE

← ANNA G.

1994

087

Marc Newson

MAGIS (ITALY)

One day, Marc Newson looked about and noticed that he was surrounded by ugly things. **'I can't stand any more ugliness!'** he thought, and proceeded to replace everything he owned with elegant and useful objects.

He designs everything: soap dishes, furniture, shoes, jewellery, bicycles, cars, aeroplanes, even spaceships! He believes that **every object can be designed to look attractive**. Not even a dish drainer should be plain or dull. Newson's **drainer** is a **prickly creature of the Australian coral reef**. But it's practical, too.

DISHES DRYING

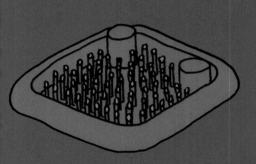

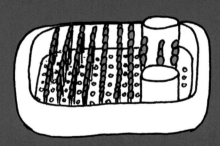

Ingo Maurer

INGO MAURER GMBH (GERMANY)

Imagine **a huge chandelier** hanging in a mansion owned by your fabulously rich aunt. To match her expensive furniture it is lavishly decorated with dazzling, dangling crystals.

Now imagine that some crazy designer takes down all the crystals and replaces them with **plain sheets of paper**. What's more, he attaches them with paper clips. And **scribbles things** like 'love you', 'you're wonderful', or 'kisses' – **in all the languages of the world**.

Your poor aunt would probably faint. But designer Ingo Maurer loves to break rules and play jokes. Zettel'z 5 is **sold with blank sheets of paper**. Maurer invites the new lamp owner to do some doodling.

BIRDIE'S NEST

005

FLYING BULBS

LAMP FROM
TOOTHPASTE
TUBES

TU-BE 1

INGO MAURER MADE
THIS LAMP TOGETHER
WITH RON ARAD
(SEE PAGE 138)

2007

Konstantin Grcic

FLOS (ITALIEN)

A lamp always has a base, an arm and a shade. Borrring... Plus they are heavy and hard to move. Can anything be done about that? Konstantin Grcic tried. He invented a lamp that's **light and handy**. 'Mayday' is **just a light-shade and a handle**, with a cable attached. You can hold it as a torch or hang it by the handle's hook. The **cable is 5 metres long**, so you can reach every dark corner. You can also stand it on its shade. Like a proper tool, it can be used in many ways and places: in the garage, the garden, or for shining under the wardrobe or duvet.

Konstantin Grcic has two rescue lamps, and he uses both. One stands by his bed; another by his front door. If an emergency strikes, he can count on them. **'Mayday' means 'help me'**, after all.

KONSTANTIN GRCIC

1999

DAD UNDER
THE CAR

LOTS OF DUST

095

Naoto Fukasawa

Naoto Fukasawa likes things to be **simple**. So simple, that with just one look you can see what they are and how they work. When he succeeds in making something that simple, he's happy.

Take a look at one of his inventions. **No doubt you know what it is.** And how to make it work. Right?

Michael Young

Michael Young claims that people are not the only ones who should benefit from stylish gadgets. Dogs deserve them, too. He designed **a funky kennel** whose elegant lines appeal to more than dogs – a fat cat, a white rabbit, a nosy ferret, and an energetic toddler love it, too.

The Dog House can stand inside, or out in the garden. It's easy to clean (a special hole in the back lets the washing water out). It comes with a set of steps and **a tail** – to announce its canine (or feline) owner.

POODLE

MICHAEL YOUNG

MAGIS (ITALY)

LITTLE TAIL

BONE VALLEY

Ronan and Erwan Bouroullec

The Bouroullec brothers observed that natural objects occur in **large quantities**. Take clouds, for example. Or snow flakes, or sand grains, or leaves, or petals. The more of a beautiful thing there is, the more beauty we can enjoy. So the brothers decided to design objects that could be multiplied and combined into bigger wholes. They invented **shelves like configurations of clouds**. When one cloud is joined by another, and another, **the room looks heavily overcast**. To escape the brooding weather, you can separate the shelves and admire the individual clouds.

The Bouroullec brothers have also made fabric clouds for wall decoration. Would you like masses of clouds in your bedroom?

CAPPELLINI (ITALY)

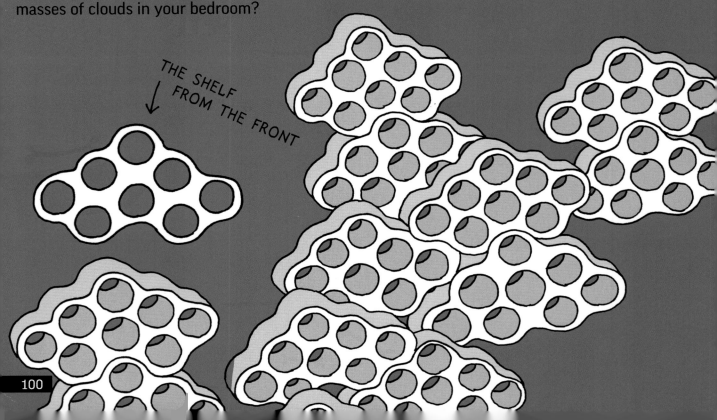

THE SHELF FROM THE FRONT

RWAN
OUROULLEC

RONAN
BOUROULLEC

MOOOI (THE NETHERLANDS)

Maarten Baas transforms furniture with fire. Seriously! He really **sets it on fire**. At first he burnt cheap chairs and tables, but later he started to set expensive works by famous designers ablaze (even some described in this book). Why does he do that? He argues that **changing an object is also designing it**. So after someone else's object is burnt by Baas, it becomes Baas's design.

To make **a burnt armchair**, Baas places a wooden frame in his garden. He pours a secret solution over it and strikes a match. The frame begins to burn, and Baas watches … and watches. When he thinks that's enough, he puts the fire out with another secret solution. When the frame is cold and dry, he coats it with transparent resin. That's why the armchair doesn't leave dirty stains on your clothes or crumble to pieces. Baas finishes it off with black leather for elegance. Finally, he numbers and signs it – **every burnt chair is unique**.

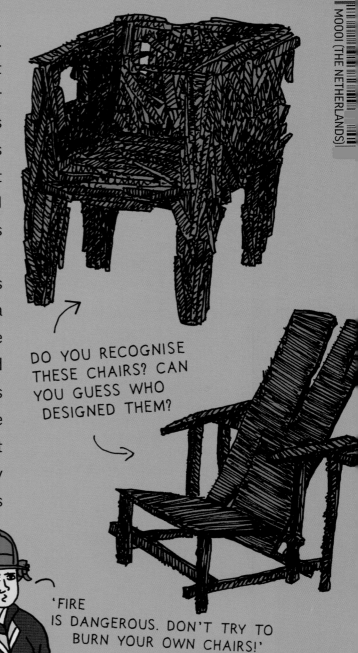

DO YOU RECOGNISE THESE CHAIRS? CAN YOU GUESS WHO DESIGNED THEM?

'FIRE IS DANGEROUS. DON'T TRY TO BURN YOUR OWN CHAIRS!'

If you've ever played cops and robbers, you know what it takes to follow someone. When you chase a robber or run from the police you need **eyes in the back of your head**. The more eyes, the better! Imagine a **big mirror ball** hung in every room you enter. No one could escape your scrutiny. No one could stalk you from behind. Tom Dixon created a **lamp** that is a big mirror ball.

He never actually dreamed of being a designer. One day, he smashed his motorbike and had no money to repair it. He had to learn how to weld – and he loved it. Now he welds whenever he can, creating things by **welding odd metal bits together**, including furniture and lamps.

WORRIED TOM DIXON

'LOOKS LIKE I NEED TO LEARN HOW TO WELD'

SMASHED BIKE

Have you ever exclaimed, **'What a gorgeous heater!'**? Well, probably not. Which is hardly surprising. But **truly amazing heaters** do exist. The most famous was designed by Joris Laarman, who called it Heat Wave. Its shapely curls tempt you to believe it's a **Rococo sculpture***.

LAARMAN HAS ALSO DESIGNED BONE CHAIR

JORIS LAARMAN

DOGS LOVE BONE CHAIR

SSSSSS

Tord Boontje

When Tord Boontje's daughter was four years old, she loved flowers, leaves and butterflies, like most little girls. So her dad designed a special lamp for her: **a hanging bouquet**.

It looks too delicate for a lamp. Could it really survive a toy aeroplane attack? And what if the skipping rope hit it? No need to worry. The lamp is **made of Tyvek, a very strong synthetic paper** that's tear-proof, heat-proof and waterproof. So the lamp can last many, many years – unless some small Tarzan decides to swing on it... At night, it conjures up **the jungle, with shadowy leaves and flowers**.

Tord Boontje wanted his lamp to be cheap, so you can buy the pieces packed in an envelope and put them together at home.

TORD
BOONTJE

BOONTJE HAS DESIGNED THESE ARMCHAIRS AND THIS TABLE, TOO

Alexander Taylor

The antlers of hunted deer used to hang proudly above the mantelpiece, as **trophies** in a position of honour. But over the years, this habit changed and they were hung in the hall, becoming **practical hangers** for hats and scarves.

Alexander Taylor has invented an ecological version – **wire antlers**. Good news for the deer!

HANGERS THAT WORK

ALEXANDER TAYLOR

FAILED HANGERS

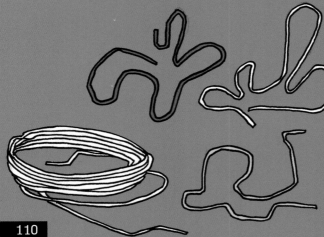

THORSTEN VAN ELTEN (UNITED KINGDOM)

2004

111

Ferruccio Laviani

To design something new, you don't have to start from scratch. You can take an old idea, shape or style, and use it in an innovative way – like the Rococo radiator**. Or a lamp by Ferruccio Laviani.

From a distance, it looks like a **300-year-old crystal lamp** in Baroque style, which means lavish in design and detail. But up close, it's **brand new**. And the crystal is actually **see-through plastic** (or transparent polycarbonate). Laviani has combined an old shape and style with a modern material to create a surprising lamp that looks as good in a palace as it does in a modern apartment.

* SHORT FOR 'BOURGEOIS', MEANING RICH, MIDDLE-CLASS, SNOBBISH

**THE ONE ON PAGE 106

'GUESS HOW OLD MY LAMP IS?'

KARTELL (ITALY)

FERRUCCIO LAVIANI

THESE LAMPS WERE ALSO DESIGNED BY LAVIANI

Karim Rashid

Designers don't only think about designing. They also have hobbies. Karim Rashid, for example, **doubles as a DJ** – he plays and samples music in clubs. For this he needs **a DJ console**. Rashid designed his console specially. It has two turntables, a mixer, and two lamps (since nightclubs are dimly-lit places). It looks like a **bulging pink blob** because Rashid loves flowing lines and the colour pink. However, if you fancy another colour, no problem – there's a cool selection on offer.

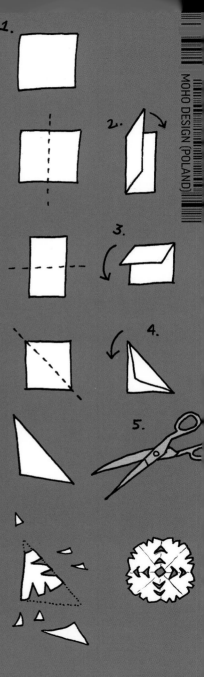

Moho Design (Magdalena Lubińska and Michał Kopaniszyn)

Take a sheet of paper. Fold it in half, and in half again, and again. Cut patterns into it with scissors. Finally, unfold the paper. Perfect! **A cut-out doily.** The DIA carpet is produced in exactly the same way, except that it's made of felt, and **cut with a laser**. Of course, you put it on the floor, not the table. The pattern resembles **a traditional Polish folk design**.

It came about when Magdalena Lubińska was decorating her flat and couldn't find a **suitable carpet**. Eventually, she decided to make one herself, along with Michał Kopaniszyn. Thus she changed from being a lawyer to a designer and carpet manufacturer.

MICHAŁ
KOPANISZYN →

2004

MAGDALENA
LUBIŃSKA →

Designed by Yves Behar, this **small green laptop** is no ordinary computer. It has a special mission: it must **assist children from poor countries** in their learning. Like any special agent, it's undergone special training and is equipped with unique gadgets. It has mastered **numerous languages**, including dialects spoken by African tribes. Its green ears hide aerials that enable **internet** connection. It has a built-in camera and microphone for **long-distance communication**.

Behar's laptop is not only highly versatile, it's also very resilient. It's shock-proof, heatproof and humidity-proof (it's meant for Africa, after all). It weighs as little as a lunch box, and takes up less space than a textbook. It can be recharged with **a few turns of the handle**, or by connecting it to a car engine. Each laptop costs only a hundred dollars to produce – around the price of a Lego set. But you can't buy it anywhere. Behar's laptops are handed out free to the children who most need them.

'EVERY CHILD SHOULD GET ONE OF THESE COMPUTERS'

ONE LAPTOP PER CHILD (USA)

YVES BEHAR

118

THESE LAPTOPS
CAN STAND DUST,
HEAT AND HUMIDITY,
SO THEY CAN BE
USED OUTDOORS

2005

Tomek Rygalik

IKER (POLAND)

Does your sofa hide things – under the seat, perhaps? Small objects do tend to find their way there, so you might want to **search your sofa for hidden treasure**, like a coin or a missing puzzle piece.

When he was designing this sofa, Tomek Rygalik remembered the **treasure hunts** of his childhood. He hid a **special storage space** in its leg. Adults can put a newspaper there, or a file, or a book. What might children put there? What a question – everything!

Hidden is not just a homely sofa. It suits public spaces, too: waiting rooms, banks, clubs, airports. It consists of **modules**, which can be joined together to fit the surroundings. For instance, a bank can arrange it like a **snake** so their customers have somewhere to sit as they wait in the queue. In a nightclub, friends can sit in a **horseshoe** so they can see one another.

RYGALIK'S SOFA CAN BE ARRANGED IN VARIOUS WAYS

LIKE A SNAKE

OR A HORSESHOE

TOMEK RYGALIK

2005

121

Malafor (Agata Kulik-Pomorska and Paweł Pomorski)

Wandering through the woods can be tiring. Sooner or later you need to look for somewhere to sit and rest. On the soft moss here ... oh, it's wet. What about that little hill? Right, it's an anthill... **A tree stump: that will do!** It makes **such a comfortable stool**, you'd happily take it home. The Malafor designers did. They took their stump home and transformed it into a stool. Just as a stump in the woods looks similar to the trees around it, the stump at home blends into its surroundings. It is wrapped in a steel sheet that mirrors nearby objects – **a camouflage stump** perhaps?

AGATA KULIK-POMORSKA

PAWEŁ POMORSKI

Hella Jongerius loves the landscape of Holland, her homeland. Out of her deep love for the vast, flat, low-lying fields called **polders***, she designed a sofa that is also **flat and vast** (330 centimetres wide, the width of two normal sofas). Like polders, her sofa comes in different colours. Green – the way polders appear in spring. Beige – the colour of ripe crops at the height of summer. Greyish-brown – the hue of newly-turned soil in autumn. And red – because in Holland, fields are always full of flowers, especially tulips. Jongerius even divided her sofa with cushions to create the patchwork effect of **the Dutch landscape**. To prevent any further doubt, she named her sofa **Polder**.

VITRA (SWITZERLAND)

HELLA JONGERIUS

JONGERIUS EVEN DESIGNED
SPECIAL BUTTONS
FOR HER POLDER SOFA

* FERTILE FIELDS LYING BELOW SEA-LEVEL. BECAUSE THEY'VE BEEN RECLAIMED FROM THE SEA, THEY NEED TO BE SECURED BY DIKES TO KEEP THE WATER BACK. ALSO, THEY NEED TO BE CONSTANTLY DRAINED WITH THE HELP OF SPECIAL CANALS AND PUMPS.

AXOR HANSGROHE (GERMANY)

Jean-Marie Massaud

Jean-Marie Massaud loves to **observe nature**. When he designed a sports stadium, he modelled it on a **volcano**. Creating an armchair, he shaped it as a **truffle** (a rare mushroom that is extremely expensive). **His tap was inspired by a waterfall.** Not only does it look like a waterfall, it also behaves like one. Cool cascades of water!

Massaud's tap uses only half the water of an ordinary tap, so each time you wash your hands under this waterfall, you're saving water!

JEAN-MARIE
MASSAUD

THE HOME WATERFALL
CAN PLUMMET
INTO
A WASHBASIN ...

... OR INTO
A BATHTUB

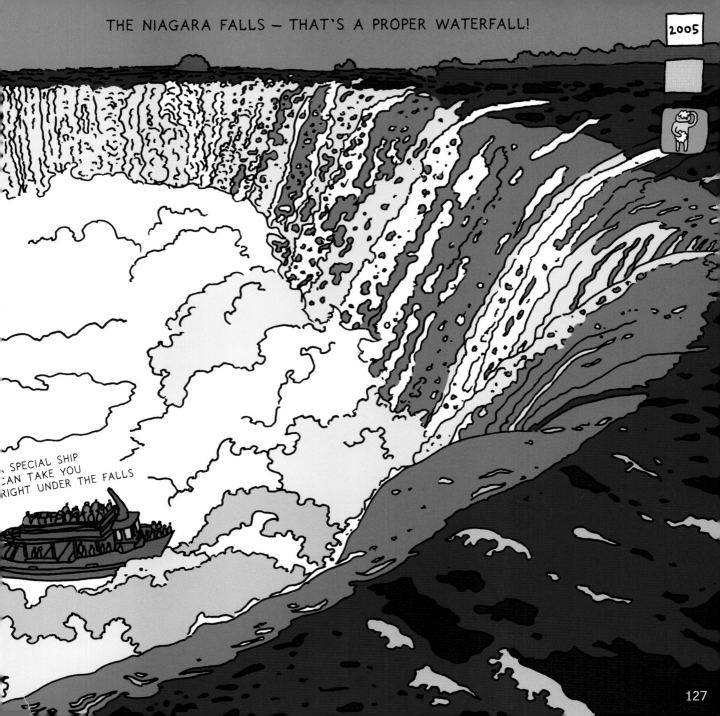

Patricia Urquiola

Other designers call Patricia Urquoila a volcano or a tornado. Why? She has a strong personality, boundless energy, and lots of excellent ideas. She also has a great sense of humour. When the Italian furniture manufacturer B&B asked her for **a sexy collection of furniture**, she patted her hips and replied that she could only offer these – her **extra kilograms**. And, indeed, she came up with **fat, feminine ottomans and sofas** with round curves and plump shapes – so nice to touch.

PATRICIA
URQUIOLA

2007

AZE Design (Anna Kotowicz-Puszkarewicz and Artur Puszkarewicz)

Every child knows how smooth and **tempting** a wall is. Especially when there's a crayon nearby. However, parents don't understand this temptation. To help both sides, Anna and Artur Puszkarewicz invented **colouring wallpaper**. You no longer have to rein-in your imagination. Your mum no longer has to despair, 'Not again! Not another pony on my newly-painted wall!' Thanks to the Puszkarewiczs' idea, **children too can be designers and be allowed to decorate walls**. The wallpaper comes in two versions: one is a meadow full of flowers; the other features ships, planes and spaceships. (They even look cool uncoloured.)

ANNA KOTOWICZ-PUSZKAREWICZ

ARTUR PUSZKAREWIC

2007

131

Inga Sempé

These days, no one is much surprised by an **adjustable table**. We all know the trick: Mum and Dad pull the table from each side and a hole appears. They slot in another piece of table top, making room to seat Grandma and Granddad, Auntie and Uncle, and all the others.

Inga Sempé wondered, if tables can be adjusted, why not lamps? Her **adjustable lamp** hangs above the table, and when the table is enlarged, the lamp can be, too. Adjusting the lamp is easier than adjusting a table, though. It resembles a pleated skirt with **vertical, stretchable folds and there is no need to slot in another piece of lamp**.

LUCEPLAN (ITALY)

INGA SEMPÉ'S LAMP STRETCHES LIKE SO

2007

INGA
SEMPÉ

133

Marcel Wanders

Marcel Wanders used to have a house with an **amazing ceiling, decorated with plaster flowers and leaves**.

He called the ceiling his 'sky garden', and was happy to see the plants grow without any wate-ring or trimming – it was enough to switch the light on to make **the plaster plants bloom**. When Wanders moved house, he missed his ceiling garden so much that he designed a special lamp with plaster plants inside. Naturally, he called it **Skygarden**.

MARCEL WANDER

2007

135

Nipa Doshi   Jonathan Levien

MOROSO (ITALY)

You might have heard of **the princess and the pea**. Have you ever wondered whether it's comfortable to sleep on a bed with so many mattresses? Well, here's your chance. Nipa Doshi and Jonathan Levien have designed a daybed that consists of **eleven colourful mattresses**.

Hans Christian Andersen's princess could feel one little pea through all the mattresses. What might **a modern princess** feel? The designers have plenty of ideas: sunglasses, scissors, a high-heeled shoe, an umbrella, a hair-dryer, a necklace, a watch, a glass – to name just a few of the objects printed on the top mattress cover.

JONATHAN LEVIEN

'WE'RE LOOKING FOR THE TRUE PRINCESS'

NIPA DOSHI

DAYBED SEEN FROM ABOVE

A GRUMPY PRINCESS

THESE THINGS ARE PRINTED ON THE MATTRESS

2008

TEUCO (ITALY)

Which is better: **a bath or a shower**? Well, it depends, don't you think? In a bath you can have a nice splash or a relaxing soak; with a shower you can have a quick and energizing wash. A shower cabinet takes up less space, but it would be great to have both. That's what Ron Arad thought, so he invented a smart **two-in-one** showerbath, which he called **'Rotator'**.

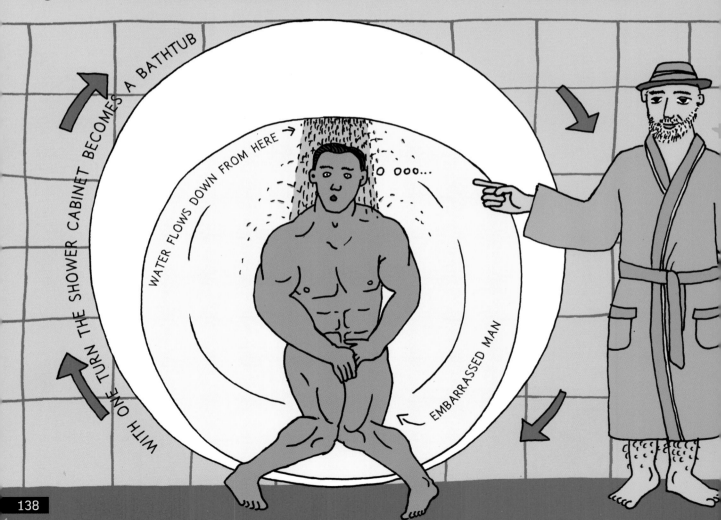

WITH ONE TURN THE SHOWER CABINET BECOMES A BATHTUB

WATER FLOWS DOWN FROM HERE

O ooo...

EMBARRASSED MAN

138

You can rotate the bathtub to change it into a shower cabinet. One more turn, and it's a bathtub again. When you want to shower, simply move the wide part of the Rotator to the top. That protects the bathroom from your enthusiastic splashes.

When you want a bubble bath, turn the Rotator upside down. Now the wide, protective part becomes a comfy tub! But how to empty a bathtub without a plug hole? It's easy: turn the Rotator once more and the water pours into a special outlet.

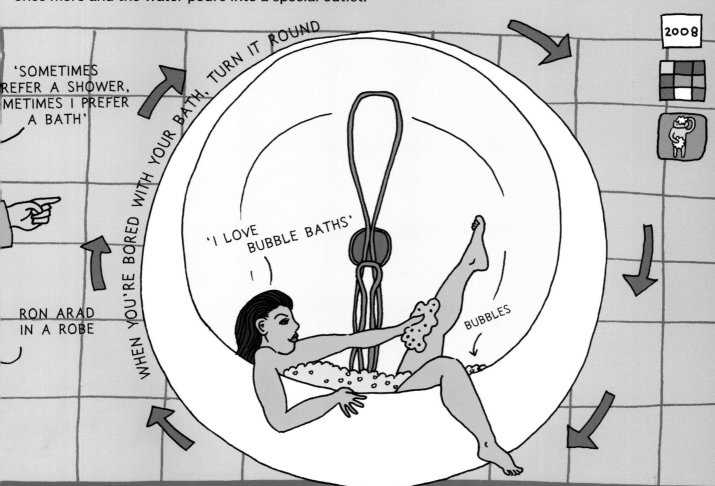

The Nendo Group (Oki Sato)

The famous **Japanese fashion designer Issey Miyake** loves creating pleated dresses and skirts. Unfortunately, **masses of pleated paper** are wasted in the process. Miyake wasn't happy about that, so he invited Oki Sato to use the paper for a piece of furniture.* Sato rolled the paper together very tightly, and then – layer by layer – he carefully cut it with scissors and peeled each layer back. He added special **resins** to make the layers **strong and sturdy**, while the pleats made the seat **soft and bouncy**. The chair looked like **a cabbage**. It's very easy to create, and Oki Sato hopes that in the future, people will be able to buy paper rolls, peel them back and make their own paper seats.

ISSEY MIYAKE MAKES BEAUTIFUL DRESSES

← ISSEY MIYAKE

SOMEONE JUST SAT ON THE CABBAGE

* THIS IS SOME MORE CREATIVE RECYCLING, LIKE THAT ON PAGE 76

140

OKI SATO

OKI SATO DEMONSTRATES HOW TO MAKE A CABBAGE CHAIR

Fabio Novembre

Fabio Novembre was wondering what kind of chairs the first humans, **Adam and Eve**, would have had. In his thought experiment, he pictured a man and a woman strolling through their garden with nothing on. He introduced into the garden his ideal chair – **Verner Panton's chair**.* You can guess the rest... If Adam and Eve had sat on Panton chairs, they would have left the imprints of their backs, bums, and legs.

Novembre created **'Her' for the woman**, and **'Him' for the man**. Sometimes people blush when they see them, but Novembre says: 'Adam and Eve did not feel ashamed; neither do my chairs.'

'WHOSE BUM IS THIS?'

*CAN YOU REMEMBER IT? IF NOT, SEE PAGE 56

FABIO NOVEMBRE

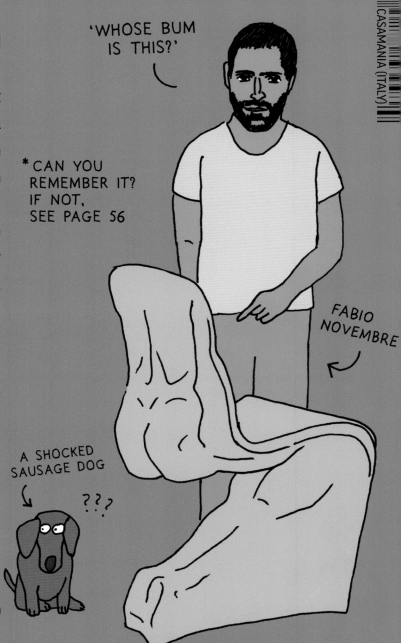

ALL WRINKLES AND FOLDS – A SHAR-PEI DOG

A SHOCKED SAUSAGE DOG

???

Do you like **skeletons**? Would your parents agree to keeping one in the hall? Does that sound weird? Well, it looks even weirder. This skeleton is not only a **mirror**, but also a **sticker**. You can stick it anywhere you wish. These designers love **bugs, skulls and other disgusting things** – and the skeleton is their favourite motif.

With such long arms it can't be a human skeleton, can it? What is it, then? A chimp or a cave man? Now, who would want to look into their own ancestor?

JOB SMEETS

STUDIO JOB

NYNKE TYNAGEL

SKULL WITH A WORM

MEGA-SPIDER

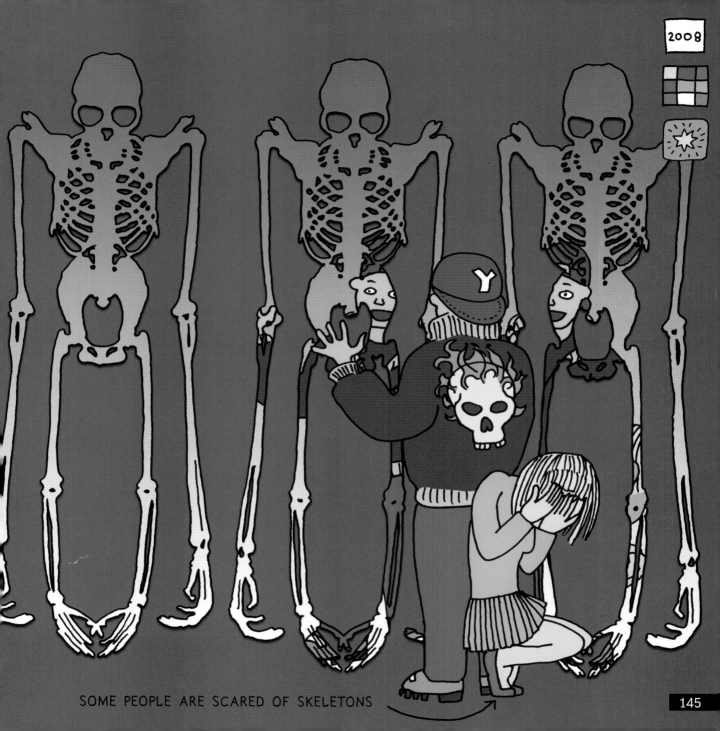

SOME PEOPLE ARE SCARED OF SKELETONS

145

WHAT ARE YOUR FAVOURITE REVOLTING THINGS?

WEREWOLF

A MAN WHO TURNS INTO A W... AT FULL MO...

MEGA SPIDER

SKULLS

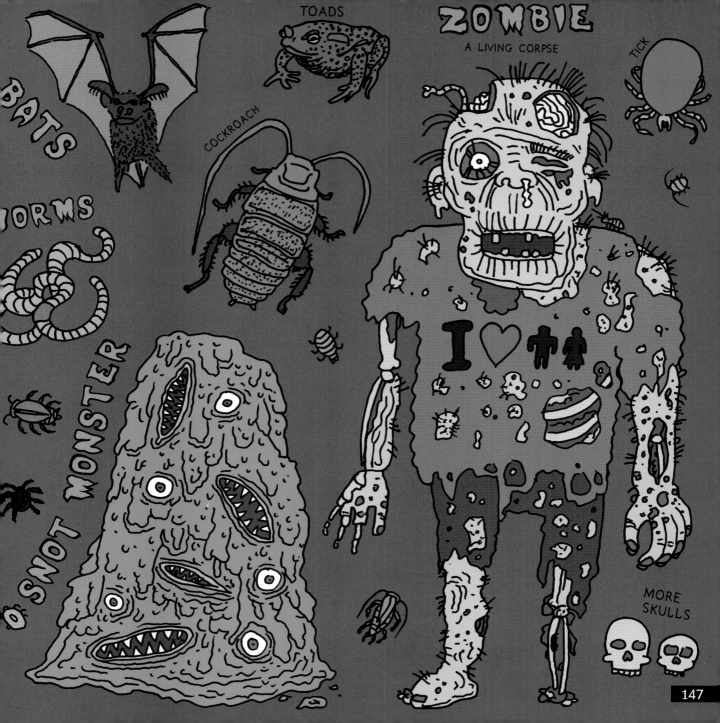

BATS

WORMS

TOADS

COCKROACH

ZOMBIE
A LIVING CORPSE

TICK

I ♥ 👨 👩

SNOT MONSTER

MORE SKULLS

147

MAGIS (ITALY)

Javier Mariscal is a designer who also draws cartoons, illustrations for children's books, and even animated films. That may explain why his furniture looks like it's straight from a comic strip. His **house for girls** is made out of **cardboard**. You buy it in parts, put it together, then colour it the way you want.

Mariscal must have asked some girls for advice, because he did a brilliant job. The house is big enough to **fit everything a small girl needs**: dolls and toys, pots and pans, a toy washing machine and a CD-player. With the door shut tight, not even a big brother can spoil the fun. The house has a chimney, flat roof, lamp above the door, windows, and plants in pots. It comes with a set of stickers: flowers, birds, ants, a dog, a cat, and a mouse. (Every proper house needs its own mouse.)

JAVIER MARISCAL HAS DESIGNED
A LOT OF THINGS FOR CHILDREN:

NIDO (NEST) 2004

A YELLOW BEAST WITH BULGING
EYES – IT COULD BE A TENT,
A SUBMARINE, A GIGANTIC BUG
OR A SEA MONSTER

2004

LADRILLOS (BRICKS)

COLOURFUL CREATURES
THAT SUPPORT SHELVES
– THEY CAN BE ARRANGED
IN DIFFERENT WAYS

A GRINNING CAT
TRANSFORMED INTO A CHAIR

2004   JULIAN

PIEDRAS (STONES)

2006

FURNITURE FOR CAVE-FAMILIES

THEY SEEM TO BE CARVED IN ROCK, BUT ACTUALLY THEY'RE MADE OF STURDY, WATERPROOF FOAM

JAVIER MARISCAL

Oskar Zięta

The Polish designer Oskar Zięta has invented and patented a new way to process metal. With the help of a laser, he cuts a shape out of **two very thin steel sheets**. Next he welds the two pieces together around the edges. Then he pumps water inside under very high pressure to create **a three-dimensional object**. Afterwards, he pours the water out, then bends the steel this way and that, until his furniture has the form he likes.

That's how these stools are made. They **look like inflated beach toys**, but are **stable and durable**. What's more, **each is unique**.

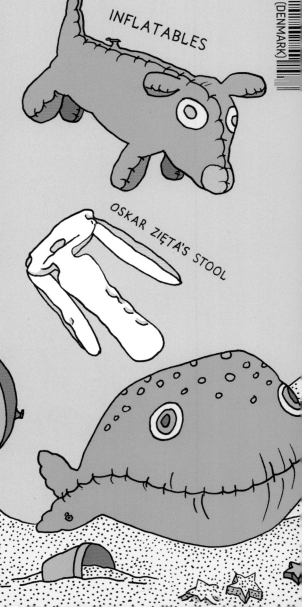

INFLATABLES

OSKAR ZIĘTA'S STOOL

Benoît Convers of the Ibride group

Do you remember what happened to Pinocchio when he didn't want to learn? He was turned into … a donkey. Maybe this strange desk was once a stubborn, lazy boy named Martin? Or maybe this donkey belonged to an artist who was always on the lookout for a flash of inspiration…

Imagination is all-important to Benoît Convers, and 'Martin' is only one of his **menagerie**: Dog Sultan is a coffee table; Doe Bambi is a chest of drawers; Bear Joe is a bookcase. How did all these animals get into Convers's head? **Straight from the woods.** He invents his furniture by observing the animals that appear in the forest around his house.

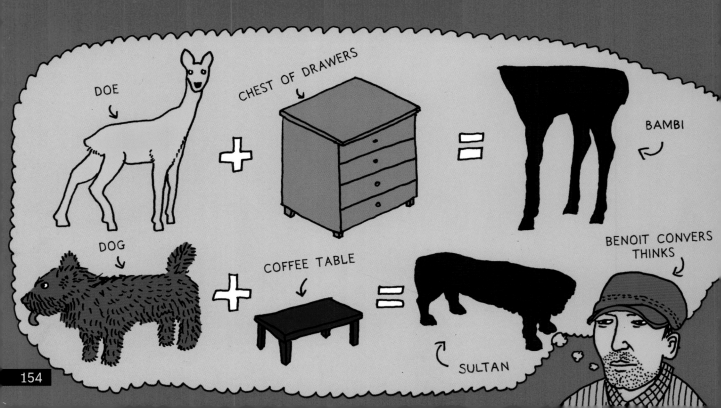

DOE

CHEST OF DRAWERS

BAMBI

DOG

COFFEE TABLE

BENOIT CONVERS THINKS

SULTAN

Philippe Nigro

No two people are alike – therefore, a single piece of furniture won't suit everyone. What is ideal for one person will be uncomfortable for another. Too hard, too soft, too long, too short, too high, too low.

Philippe Nigro has **designed a seating system** that can be put together like a **jigsaw puzzle** to suit you and anyone else in your family. How does it work?

Imagine a couple in a furniture shop. They're in love and can't stop gazing into each other's eyes. For their sofa, they choose two elements that will face one other. The man is big and tall, so he takes a firm, wide piece. The woman is short and doesn't like her legs to dangle; she takes a shorter, softer piece. Then the two lovers are joined by their family – dad, mum, sister, brother – and each finds what suits them. When they've chosen, the shop-assistant assembles all the pieces into one comfortable sofa. 'Confluences' help you to **create furniture that's truly your own**.

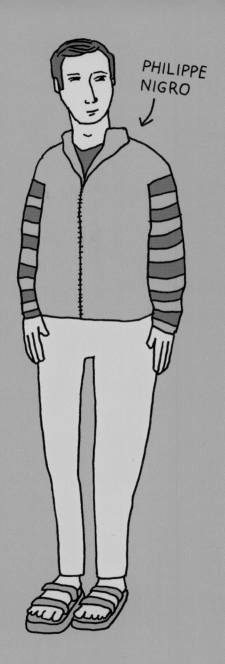

PHILIPPE NIGRO

SOFA SEEN
FROM ABOVE

2009

157

Designers can be inspired by just about anything – even by **six women who lived about 450 years ago**. Jaime Hayon likes to go back in time, so when he was asked to invent chairs for an English firm, he gladly travelled back to the Tudor age. There he met **Henry VIII**, who had the bad habit of changing wives too often. He got married six times. Two of his wives were executed.

Jaime Hayon looked at the portraits of the **king's six wives** – at first they seemed identical. Identical clothes and hairstyles, painted identically. But on closer inspection, he could see that they all differed. That's how he designed his chairs. At first they seem the same, but look more closely and you'll notice that their details differ – the quilted seats, and the colour of their upholstery and legs.

HENRY VIII (1509–1547), THE SECOND MONARCH OF THE HOUS OF TUDOR

CATHERINE OF ARAGON

ANNE BOLEYN

JANE SEYMOUR

ANNE OF CLEVES

KATHRYN HOWARD

KATHERINE PARR

2009

JAIME
HAYON

Stefano Giovannoni

These **friendly monkeys** look like toys – but they're not! They're **kitchen gadgets**: salt and pepper shakers, bottle stoppers, corkscrews, salt and pepper grinders, timers, toothpick holders. Stefano Giovannoni loves such weird combinations: everyday objects transformed into amusing toys. His monkey tribe was invented in cooperation with **the National Palace Museum in Taipei, Taiwan**. In the Chinese culture **monkeys are very important**.

STEFANO
GIOVANNON
AND
THE MONKE
CORKSCRE

CRAZY
MONKEYS

OO ... OO ...
OO! OO!
OOOO!

The Front group (Sofia Lagerkvist, Charlotte von der Lancken, Anna Lindgren and Katja Sävström)

MOROSO (ITALY)

Look at these three sofas. The first is covered with a draped fabric, the second is a pile of cushions, and the third is made of wood. In front of them lies a carpet that catches the sun shining through the window. Right? Well, wrong!

The cushions, fabric, and wood are **photographic images printed on items of furniture**. Actually, these sofas are flat and soft, with nothing lying on them. What about the carpet? Late at night it will still show the sun's rays. **How come?** The designers from the Swedish group **Front** wanted to play a joke on those of us who believe everything we see.

THIS IS NOT A DRAPED FABRIC

THIS IS NOT A PILE OF CUSHIONS

THIS IS NOT WOOD

THIS CARPET IS NOT FOLDED HERE AND THERE ARE NO SUN'S RAYS ON IT

THE FRONT GROUP

SOFIA LAGERKVIST

ANNA LINDGREN

CHARLOTTE VON DER LANCKEN

KATJA SÄVSTRÖM

2009

SOFA COVER

163

This English edition first published in 2011 by Gecko Press
PO Box 9335, Marion Square, Wellington 6141, New Zealand
info@geckopress.com

Text and concept: Ewa Solarz
Illustrations and design: Aleksandra and Daniel Mizieliński
© Wydawnictwo Dwie Siostry, Warsaw, Poland 2010
Translation from the Polish © Elżbieta Wójcik-Leese 2011

National Library of New Zealand Cataloguing-in-Publication Data

Solarz, Ewa.
D.E.S.I.G.N. English
D.E.S.I.G.N. / by Ewa Solarz ; illustrated by Aleksandra & Daniel Mizieliński ; translated by Elżbieta Wójcik-Leese.
ISBN 978-1-877467-83-7
1. Design—History—Juvenile literature. 2. Designers—Juvenile literature. 3. House furnishings—Design—Juvenile literature.
[1. Design—History. 2. Designers. 3. House furnishings—Design.]
I. Mizieliński, Aleksandra. II. Mizieliński, Daniel. III. Title.
745.409—dc 22

This publication has been subsidized
by the Polish Book Institute
© Poland Translation Programme

For more curiously good books, visit www.geckopress.com

Thank you to Marta Suchodolska, my colleague at domplusdom.pl, for her help, support and patience during the writing of this book.

Thank you to Asia and Jacek Rzyski for persuading me to write D.E.S.I.G.N.
Ewa Solarz